HOUSE MOUSE

Michael Hall

Greenwillow Books
An Imprint of HarperCollinsPublishers

For Kim, Amy, and Jenna Cain

House Mouse. Copyright © 2021 by Michael Hall. All rights reserved. Manufactured in Italy. For information address HarperCollins Children's Books, a division of HarperCollins Publishers, 195 Broadway, New York, NY 10007. www.harpercollinschildrens.com. The art consists of digitally combined collages of painted and cut paper. The text type is 24-point Avenir Next. Library of Congress Cataloging-in-Publication Data is available. ISBN 978-0-06-286619-6 (hardback) 21 22 23 24 25 RTLO 10 9 8 7 6 5 4 3 2 1 First Edition Greenwillow Books

One chilly morning,

a mouse traveled over a hill,

across a river,

and into a wild asparagus patch,
where she found something remarkable.

It was warm and welcoming.

So . . .  the mouse made a stove

to mark the spot
where the chilliness wasn't.

One day, a hungry fox
chased the mouse

past a forest

and in and out of a valley.

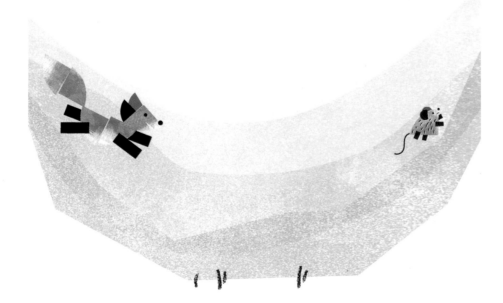

All of a sudden,
the fox stopped in its tracks.

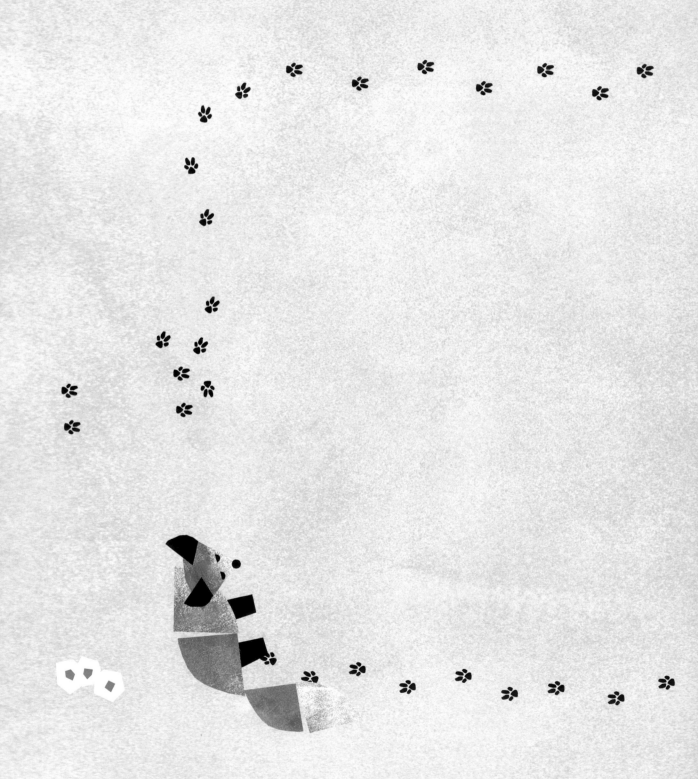

The mouse was safe.

So . . . TAP TAP TAP
the mouse made a floor

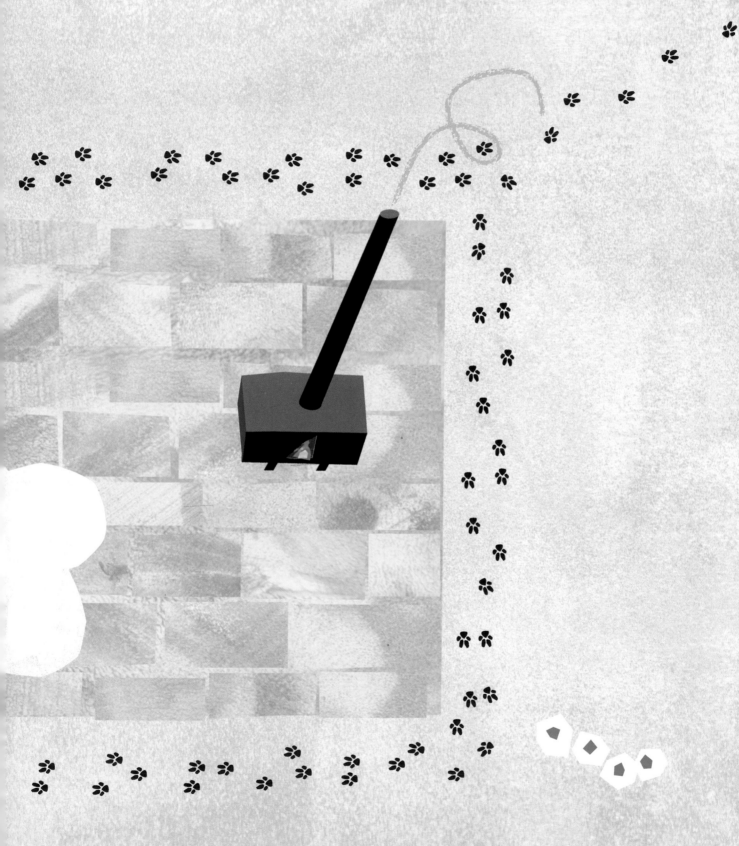

to mark the spot
where the fox wouldn't go.

During a big storm,

the mouse scampered along a slippery wall

and through a deep puddle.

But when she hopped onto her floor,
it was peaceful and dry.

So . . . THUMP THUMP THUMP

the mouse made a roof

to mark the spot
where the rain didn't fall.

For many days,
the mouse lived happily
on a steady diet
of asparagus soup.

One night, the mouse heard a sound.

KNOCK   KNOCK   KNOCK

But nothing was there.

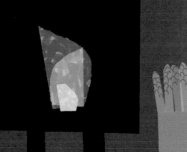

She heard it again
the next day.

KNOCK KNOCK KNOCK

Still, nothing was there.

So, the mouse made a door

SQUEAK   CREAK   BUMP

to mark the spot . . . BANG   TAP   THUMP

where the knocking had been.

And then she opened it.

"Please come in!"
she said to the
two tired travelers
huddled outside.

That evening . . .

CHOP CHOP CHOP

the new friends made
a delicious vegetable soup.

At its best,
it was a welcoming place,
and the house mouse wanted
everyone to know it.

And she still does.